NORTON SAVES THE DAY

by Bernadette Kelly

illustrated by Liz Alger

Picture Window Books
Minneapolis, Minnesota

First published in the United States in 2010
by Picture Window Books,
151 Good Counsel Drive, P.O. Box 669
Mankato, Minnesota 56002
www.picturewindowbooks.com

First published in Australia by Black Dog Books in 2008

Library of Congress Cataloging-in-Publication Data
Kelly, Bernadette.
    Norton saves the day / by Bernadette Kelly; illustrated by
Liz Alger.
    p. cm. — (Pony tales)
    ISBN 978-1-4048-5505-2 (library binding)
    [1. Ponies—Fiction. 2. Horses—Training—Fiction. 3. Behavior—
    Fiction. 4. Humorous stories.] I. Alger, Liz, ill. II. Title.
PZ7.K2927No 2010
[Fic]—dc22   2008053813

Summary: Although she thinks her pony is perfect, Molly follows
her mother's suggestion and enrolls naughty Norton in riding
school.

Creative Director: Heather Kindseth
Graphic Designer: Emily Harris

Printed in the United States of America.

Table of Contents

Meet Your Pony Pals

Norton

Molly

Isabell

Mom

Mrs. Withers

Chapter 1

Norton's Lesson

It was a school break, and I had nothing to do. Luckily, Norton was there to hang out with.

"Your pony was in the barn again this morning," said Mom. "That's the third time he got out of the corral this week."

"Norton must be opening the corral gate all by himself," I said. "What a clever pony."

"What a *naughty* pony," said Mom. "He got into that new bag of oats. It's just lucky I found him before he made himself sick."

"Maybe he's hungry," I said.

"Maybe he's bored," said Mom.

"But how can he be bored? He's got me," I said.

"You know how bored you get during a school break?" asked Mom. "Well, Norton is on a permanent school break. He needs a challenge."

"School break. That's it! I just need to take Norton to a riding school!" I said.

Chapter 2

First Lesson

Mom called the Hayfield Riding
School. They said I could come in that
morning. They were having special
lessons during school break.

I could hardly wait. Riding school
would be great for Norton. I just hoped
that the other riders wouldn't be too
jealous when they saw my clever pony.

Luckily, Hayfield was just a short ride
away.

But it took longer than I thought to get there. We had to stop on the way a few times to rest and have a snack.

"You smart pony," I said. "Of course you need to keep up your strength for school today, don't you?"

We were only a little bit late. It was
nice of the others to wait for us. I think
some of them might have been a little
worried about Norton and me being the
best at the lesson.

"We're happy to stay at your beginners' level," I told the nearest rider. Her name was Isabell.

Then I offered to help the instructor, Mrs. Withers, teach the class. Norton and I are always happy to help out whenever we can.

Mrs. Withers began the lesson with a safety talk. "Make sure you check that the girth is properly tightened. A loose girth can be very dangerous."

Norton and I showed them just how dangerous.

Then we all lined up. Of course, Norton and I were first.

"Trot," said Mrs. Withers.

Norton did a very good job of clearing a path for the others.

Norton doesn't like to be crowded.
When Isabell rode her pony up close
to us, Norton put his ears back. And,
well, Isabell should have been paying
attention.

I sure hope Isabell's ankle gets better soon. It was a shame she had to leave the lesson early. Just when we were having so much fun.

Norton was so sad that Isabell was leaving that he kicked up his heels as if to say, "Please come back."

Mrs. Withers didn't understand. She thought he was being naughty.

It was a short ride to the cross-country course. The sun was shining on Norton's glossy coat, and I saw Mrs. Withers admiring him as she walked beside us. *She probably wants to buy him,* I thought.

"This pony is not for sale," I whispered into Norton's ear.

Jumping

Poor Norton got very upset about Mrs. Withers wanting to buy him. Sometimes I forget what a sensitive pony he is.

"We'll start with an easy fence," said
Mrs. Withers. "Who wants to go first?"

Everybody looked worried, so I
thought I would help them out.

"I will," I said.

"Come on, Norton," I said. "This one is easy."

Just as Norton reached the fence, something spooked him. I think it might have been a poisonous snake or something.

I told Mrs. Withers about the
dangerous snake that had slithered away,
but she just smiled and nodded.

"If the pony hesitates," said Mrs. Withers, "the rider must be persistent. The pony will go over the jump when he realizes that there is nothing to fear. This is a tried-and-true training method."

I was still sure there was a snake.

More Tricks

At the second jump, Mrs. Withers said,
"Ditches can sometimes be a problem.
An open hole in the ground can look
scary for both horse and rider. The trick is
to keep your head up."

At the third jump, Mrs. Withers said, "This jump is called an apex. It can be tricky, so it's important to plan your approach."

Norton had a plan, but it didn't seem to be the same as mine.

The fourth jump looked really hard.

"The pony must learn to go into the water jump," said Mrs Withers. "If he hesitates, the rider must be patient and keep trying until they are successful."

"Norton," I yelled. "That wasn't funny." Even though everyone was laughing.

Everything was going wrong. I wished I'd never brought Norton to riding school.

"I am going home," I told Mrs. Withers.

"Molly Baxter," she said with a frown, "you are not going anywhere until you teach that naughty pony some manners."

Naughty? Norton? Everybody was nodding.

I was shocked! Did Mrs. Withers and the others really think my Norton was a naughty pony?

I shook my head. I just couldn't
believe it.

I loved Norton, and Norton loved me.
He wasn't being naughty. He was just
very smart.

But Mrs. Withers was right about one thing. I couldn't leave yet. Not until my pony had learned the day's lesson.

A good trainer must never give up.

·········· ✳ Chapter 5 ✳ ··········

Stop!

The showjumping lesson was my last chance. I had to show Mrs. Withers and the other riders that Norton really was a good pony.

I rode into the ring. So far, so good.

We trotted in a circle. Then I pointed
Norton toward the first fence. Norton
had his ears pricked up. He was
concentrating. I was too.

"Please, Norton," I said. "Do it for
me."

But Norton was going too fast. If he didn't slow down we wouldn't make the turn. I could feel everyone watching.

The turn was too tight.

Norton skidded, and my foot came out of the stirrup. I bounced. I tried to find the stirrup with my foot. I began to slip from the saddle. I tried to kick my other foot free of its stirrup, but it was stuck.

I was stuck hanging upside down. Norton was still running. If I hit the ground in this position, I would be dragged along on my head.

I waited for my life to flash before my eyes, but all I could think of was that I hadn't brushed my teeth that morning.

"STOOOOOPPPPP!" I yelled finally.

For the first time in his whole life, Norton obeyed. Norton. My champion. My good boy. I was so excited. Norton had saved my life.

Mrs. Withers came running up to us.
I picked myself up and shook the dust off
my jodhpurs.

There was a strange noise ringing in
my ears. Could it be? Yes! It was the other
riders cheering for Norton.

"You are lucky your pony was listening," said Mrs. Withers. "He saved you from a very nasty accident."

I hugged Norton hard. "I am very lucky to have him," I told Mrs. Withers. "He's my best friend."

After the showjumping lesson, we
put our ponies in the corral while we sat
down to eat our lunch. Everyone was
talking about Norton.

"Training a horse is a big job," I told them. "It takes time and dedication. So it's lucky for me that Norton learns fast. Um, wait a minute."

The horses were bolting through the open gate. Norton must have let them out.

"What is it? What is it, boy?" I asked him.

If there's one thing I know about Norton, it is that he never does anything without a reason. Maybe the poisonous snake had come back to bite our ponies?

That's what it was. My brave Norton
had helped all the ponies to escape.
What quick thinking!

I gave him a pat and whispered in his
ear, "Norton, you are my clever pony and
you have saved the day — again!"

✻The End✻

HORSE
❋ FUN FACTS ❋

❋ Most horses have brown eyes to match the color
   of their skin. Light-colored eyes are found only
   in spotted horses, albino horses, and a few other
   breeds.

❋ The hands have it! The height of a horse is
   measured in hands. One hand is equal to
   four inches.

❋ At maturity, a horse is expected to be at least
   14.2 hands high. If it is under this height, it is
   considered a pony.

❋ In horses, spots and stripes go together. Most
   spotted horses with spotted coats have striped
   hooves.

❋ Most horses sleep standing up. It is a natural
   instinct. By sleeping in a standing position, wild
   horses can make a quick escape when in danger.

✳ Horses usually give birth at night. It is the time when a herd is least likely to be on the move.

✳ Most of the time a horse's ears point in the direction it is looking. If the ears are pointing in two different directions, the eyes are looking at two different things. And if the ears are pointed back, watch out! The horse is probably angry.

ABOUT THE AUTHOR

While growing up, Bernadette Kelly desperately wanted her own horse. Although she rode other people's horses, she didn't get one of her own until she was a grown-up. Many years later, she is still obsessed with horses. Luckily, she lives in the country where there is plenty of room for her four-legged friends. When she's not writing or working with her horses, Bernadette takes her two children to pony club competitions.

ABOUT THE ILLUSTRATOR

Liz Alger loves horses so much that she left suburbia to live in the rambling outskirts of Melbourne, Australia. Her new home provided plenty of room to indulge in her passion. Her love of animals, horses in particular, shines through in the delightful and humorous illustrations of Norton, the naughty pony, in the Pony Tales series.

GLOSSARY

apex (AY-peks)—a type of fence that a horse jumps over. It is shaped like a V.

corral (kuh-RAL)—a fenced-in area

girth (GURTH)—the thick strap attached to the saddle. It goes under the horse's belly.

jodhpurs (JOD-purz)—pants worn for horseback riding

persistent (pur-SIS-tent)—something that continues steadily even if there are obstacles

saddle (SAD-uhl)—a seat that goes on a horse

stirrup (STUR-uhp)—a loop that hangs from the saddle where the rider puts his or her foot

trot (TROT)—when a horse goes faster than walking but is not quite running

DISCUSSION QUESTIONS

1. Have you ever ridden a horse? Would you like to? Discuss your answer.

2. Molly doesn't think Norton is naughty at all. Do you think Norton is naughty or clever? Why?

3. Were you surprised when Norton finally listened to Molly? Explain your answer.

WRITING PROMPTS

1. Write a paragraph about your favorite animal. Be sure to include why you picked the animal.

2. Molly's mom says Norton is bored. Make a list of five things you do when you are bored.

3. At the end of the story, the other riders cheer for Molly and Norton. Write a paragraph describing how you think that made Molly feel.

✷ Take Another Ride ✷ with Norton

✷

. . . .

Norton is a naughty pony. Everyone thinks so.
Well, everyone except his owner, Molly. She thinks
Norton is the most perfect pony in the whole
world, no matter what kind of trouble he causes!

. . . .

✷

Pony Tales